MW01129389

The Color of Hope

And other short stories...

by

RAYMOND ALVIN SMITH

Bloomington, IN Milton Keynes, UK

AuthorHouse™
1663 Liberty Drive, Suite 200
Bloomington, IN 47403
www.authorhouse.com
Phone: 1-800-839-8640

AuthorHouse™ UK Ltd.
500 Avebury Boulevard
Central Milton Keynes, MK9 2BE
www.authorhouse.co.uk
Phone: 08001974150

First published by AuthorHouse 9/14/2006

ISBN: 1-4208-5532-8 (e)
ISBN: 1-4208-5531-X (sc)

Library of Congress Control Number: 2005904142

Printed in the United States of America
Bloomington, Indiana

This book is printed on acid-free paper.

Juanita Aljuwani-Smith: Author Photograph

Leonard Bethle: Cover Illustration

TABLE OF CONTENTS

THE COLOR OF HOPE

The loss was not spectacular. He merely felt the solid impact of a fist against his jaw, like a moving shadow of a devastating authority. Numbness started from the center of his back and traveled down his legs.

He was surprised at the absence of pain and a feeling of weightlessness. He seemed to be outside his body, watching himself from a distance, lying there in the center of the ring.

When he saw his manager's face up close and frowning, mouth moving, the words could not be heard. Then he drifted off, remembering nothing until the next morning, when he awoke with a stinging headache.

Vague reflections of the nature of his art came to mind. It was like a familiar dream somehow unsettling. He wondered if he'd ever had a fighter's heart or sufficient ability.

Now he felt alone as he did when running the back roads of the countryside or on quiet city streets, running in solitude to increase his stamina; alone as when shadow boxing in front of a mirror or pounding the speed bag, listening to the rat-a-tat rhythm of fist against leather, leather against wood, a monotonous cadence, almost hypnotic, producing a tranquility that diminishes concentration.

When he was first approached and told of his potential, he thought he was being buttered up, a prelude to some sort of contrived rip-off. What was the pitch? When would he be pressured into giving up something they wanted?

But all they said-actually they said a lot-was that he could go far, be a class fighter, a heavy weight contender, maybe more. Fame and respect, money and recognition, even adoration could be his.

"But I'm only a wrestler!" he protested.

"That's Okay, we'll build from there."

They looked him over as if inspecting a prized gladiator prospect, a rough thoroughbred needing only proper training.

He would be the carrier of a message; a symbol of the greatness of his people; a reminder to the others of a universal genetic reality.

He had only the vague notion what they were talking about. All that registered was their irrepressible enthusiasm and almost sensual delight in his being. Strength and size was what he'd had from birth, but they said it would be enough. Training would develop to clear sharpness, the reality of his inherent ability. It would provide cut and polish as to an unfashioned diamond. The essence was never truly grasped to the point of understanding. It was flattering and compelling, and he had no other dream and therefore nothing to lose. It gave focus and meaning to the only talents he possessed. What else was size and strength good for?

Training began when certain papers were signed and pocket money provided. Calisthenics and shadow boxing seemed to magnifide a certain awkwardness, lack of style. The fluid motions observed in other fighters seemed unrelated to his attempts. He wondered if he would ever be able to deliver a smooth, stinging jab, followed by an effective combination of hooks and crosses, the stock-in-trade of the good ones.

From the beginning punching with the right hand showed some promise, a natural flow. Plus power. But when it didn't connect he was vulnerable to an assortment of counter responses, leaving him dazed and bewildered.

Four years of fighting as an amateur revealed limited ability but steady progress. He lost his first bout by a split decision then reeled off twenty straight wins including twelve knockouts. This convinced his handlers he needed a new, catchy handle. They chose the name Palomino because of his natural blond hair and muscular body responding to training, and a bronze color, the gift of the sun.

With three additional knockouts, clean and impressive, media attention, which had been sporadic, blossomed into a carnival-like frenzy, spawning the catch phrase, Palomino Power, suggesting invincibility. To Palomino it was all incomprehensible, this strange attention. But why blow it? Enjoy it while you can, he told himself. It could end tomorrow.

Often on quiet afternoons, with training over, the team gathered to watch old fight films. It was history and instruction combined.

Palomino's favorites were Archie Moore and Sugar Ray Robinson. He loved Moore's way of slipping punches, countering in the clinches and his wicked left hook. And no one matched Sugar Ray's masterful mixture of boxing and punching power. His manager preferred Jack Dempsey and Rocky Marciano and saw Palomino's style as similar. A protesting Palomino couldn't see the slightest resemblance and said as much. Soon only movies of white fighters were brought to camp. Palomino didn't protest, he simply wondered if he really was the one to fulfill their vision. The idea was alluring and soon began to inflame his training. Every hour in the gym was accompanied by intense enthusiasm. He had the feeling of becoming more than he thought possible, of being driven by unknown forces penetrating his meager talents and transforming them into something remarkable; the feeling of becoming the potential hero they dreamed of.

Training camp became an arena of glorification, an extension of the rituals of the game. Crowds gathered as if at a picnic. Media interviewed, made predictions, speculated. Fathers brought their sons to shake his hand; mothers wanted to feel his biceps, bake him pies. Palomino enjoyed most of all the attention of the high–classed females who followed the game. They accepted him as a natural object of their adoration. He was, in some peculiar fashion, "theirs".

When the training was held outside, sports writers and paid attendees came like tourists to view a natural wonder. Photo sessions and autographing followed. A particular young blond who came often had this need to touch any part of him, being particularly fond of his knees. She talked about blood and brute power; likened him to policemen who were equally attractive for the same reason-an ability to overcome those others who were so threatening and who provided a feeling of security.

Having become the media's darling, turning pro was only a formality. His first fight was a stunning eight round knockout, left hook working to perfection. Believing the dream seemed even more possible.

His opponent, an aging Mexican who could still fight, also had cleverness going for him. During the clinches difficiencies of manhood and lack of virility were blown in Palomino's ear. Emasculating phrases calculated to unnerve the gullible.

"After I kick your butt you ain't never gonna get hard again." Having been warned of verbal warfare, the bait was refused.

Cool and controlled he dissected the Mexican's style; a low crouch, elbows bent, both hands close to his face, moving slowly to the left and then suddenly straight forward; double left hooks to the face and body then quickly out and moving left again.

Every fighter lives within the dictates of an individual style revealed through repetition. By the fifth round, Palomino knew. The Mexican's left hook, which could have been deadly earlier in his career, no longer had power. And his timing was a joke. Whenever he was about to unload, his chin raised slightly and jutted right, a peculiarity also observed by Palomino's handlers. They agreed his left hook should do the job, and in the eighth round, it happened.

He remembered the movies of Ezzard Charles knocking out Bob Satterfield. Charles had described the blow as a perfect left hook, clearly unexpected, traveling a short distance and exploding with devastating effectiveness. Satterfield went down smoothly, almost peacefully, without a thought, and lay on the canvas. Such was the power of a heavyweight who could punch.

The Mexican hit the canvas with greater reluctance, hands searching the air for something to grasp; trying to stop the inevitable.

Three days later when he arrived at the gym, movies of the fight were already available.

"Come and watch!" his manager had said. "Now that's a left hook!"

Palomino viewed the movies and noted with pride that the hooks were similar. He relived the moment, imitating his own movement, feeling the power of a phantom blow, delivered in the confines of the viewing room.

The delight of his handlers was absolute. Palomino began to visualize the fulfillment of the dream. Any remaining doubt disappeared and, like the images of the Mexican lying in stillness, faded away.

His handlers had visions of their own,- Palomino, fighting at Madison Square Garden, in with a name fighter, a contender, on the under card of maybe a championship fight. International recognition. A big payday!

At one hundred and ninety-five pounds Palomino had fought heavyweights and light-heavies, but none had a great reputation, But the next time out that's exactly what he got, a black fighter ranked number seven. "Lucky Seven," his manager said.

But even with the excitement of such an opportunity his team appeared apprehensive.

They spoke of flaws that could prove fatal, a tendency to lose concentration when not being pressed; inappropriate use of the jab, pawing instead of stabbing like a spear;

hesitating before throwing a right cross, weak points which the good fighter could exploit.

"Don't worry" his manager kept repeating, and Palomino, if not worried, surely began to wonder. *Am I in over my head? Is the guy too good for me?*

But training was going well. Working with better sparing partners provided a gauge of his true ability which he could now evaluate for himself. Any reservations about his talents never blossomed into genuine doubt.

Speed was improving, combinations natural and most important, an evolving ability to decipher the style of other fighters, provided sufficient reason for confidence.

He enjoyed studying the mannerism of different fighters, different boxing styles, the mechanics of punching power, everything.

This appreciation of the art culminated in an admiration of the really good ones and the awareness of his ability. He began to realize he was one of them, a pro class fighter. He knew it, even if his handlers were nervous.

They hadn't made him. He was a product of his own heart. They could only vicariously identify with his evolution. He was like a dancer who worked at learning new steps, different routines, from the inside out, gradually unfolding until, behold! Here I am!

He was a fighter in a manner only other fighters could understand. Because he knew what he was, their doubts had little significance. He knew! That was enough.

The plan was to gain respect early with a demonstration of Palomino Power. Utilize the right cross; let him know the left hook. Tie him up with strength of arms and shoulders. Show your ability to slip a punch. Absorb a blow when necessary. Above all, show the crowd what you are.

The first three rounds were close; by the fourth, Palomino had the edge, scoring effectively to the body with combinations that had the crowd chanting, "Palomino! Palomino! Palomino!"

The cheering was intoxicating, He felt stronger than ever. Each move was orchestrated as if determined by some internal, automatic devise, incapable of error. The final movement came without conscious direction. When his opponent fell, he cheered as if seated in the front row with the spectators. And when his handlers raised him up on their shoulders he felt like a king!

Palomino ranked number five when he fought again. Now he was the contender; expected to win. He reeled off another string of victories, showing authentic boxing skill and punching power, delighting his supporters, silencing all criticism. He was definitely the genuine article. Fulfilling the dream seemed possible.

Fights became more difficult as he moved up in ranking until be was rated number three. Only one fighter stood between him and a championship bout; a young black prospect from Philly, also labeled a comer, fast and clean living with a good right. The fight was scheduled for July Fourth to augment the traditional celebration. Media interviews became pointed, questions searching.

"Do you enjoy knocking out people?"

"What's the most difficult aspect of training?"

"How does it feel to be the current white hope?"

His manager intercepting the questions, insisted that Palomino was simply an average American with boxing talents, working hard and living the American Dream.

On the Fourth of July Palomino Power became a receding shooting star unable to sustain the brightness or continue the climb.

After the loss, he was unable to be part of the public explanation offered by his handlers.

"He carried the fight for five rounds."

"It was a lucky punch, one mistake was all."

But he knew better. His opponent's style was obvious, even simple, which may have been why it worked so well. And Palomino could do nothing effective against it. The black fighter, instead of moving in and out, stayed two inches beyond the reach of Palomino's jab, avoided the right cross by ducking under it and landed with regularity his own counter blows.

Palomino's blows that caused the crowd to roar, landed harmlessly on shoulders and arms. The right hand landed occasionally but without authority. It was like trying to unite with an illusive specter. Well-timed blows seemed to pass through his opponent without effect.

Palomino's growing frustration went unnoticed by his corner. He seemed to be focused and in command. And there was no apparent loss of style or determination. Clearly lacking was effectiveness. Nothing worked. His best was simply not good enough.

When the end came, there was shock, disbelief, rage and disappointment among the handlers.

In the weeks that followed, they talked of regrouping, correcting mistakes. The handlers still had hope.

Palomino said he would think about it. But he knew. Watching the movies of the fight only confirmed a critical reality. Fighters are not born superior regardless of genetic certainty. Some are better than others. Fighters enter the ring carrying only individual hearts, without the support of cultural history or genetic heritage. They enter alone, fight alone, and lose alone.

Palomino fought three times after the loss, winning mediocre decisions, impressing no one. Citing miscalculations and overrating, the media backed off. There were no more offers of sexual favors or pies baked special. Fathers looked elsewhere for support and confirmation.

When Palomino stopped showing up for training no one called. He heard there was a new hope with a winning smile, olive complexion, and black wavy hair. He would eventually be called Romeo-loved by all.

Palomino went back to using his nick name Dickie, which he liked only slightly better than Richard. He grew long hair, wore dark glasses, and worked as a bouncer in an unpretentious cowboy bar in central Texas without being recognized.

He continued to enjoy running and discovered that even Texas had quiet wooded areas. Now he could jog without an entourage and only the sound of woodland creatures as company. No longer occupying the pedestal of their hopes, even the silence was a joy. He had thought that hero-ship, once bestowed, could be retained forever.

One day he received a letter. Someone had returned an autograph, on a card, with a note, citing disappointment and betrayal. He kept the card in a wallet containing little else. Often he stared at the words of praise and his signature, hardly recognizing it as his own. He wondered about the sender's disappointment. What was his failure? How could he, alone, be expected to sustain their myth of collective superiority?

When he married he encouraged his children's early interest in hockey. He never spoke of his past; only that on the hard, blue ice the myths were real, their kind of life, and heroes and hope were genuine.

LOW BOY'S DAY AT THE BEACH

Low Boy, a half grown chimpanzee, had gotten use to his position near the bottom of the hierarchy of power and prestige, being deprived of any sexual activity, eating leftovers and generally enduring posturing attitudes and bad intentions from the Alpha chimps who ran the show.

It wasn't so much that he was disliked. Ever so often the Alphas would actually groom him, picking lice and other vermin from his ears and between his toes, and fluffing up his fur. It made him feel good, accepted, even loved. But there remained the code of the troop-only Alphas could procreate; only they had the required genetic stuff capable of insuring the troop's survival. Alphas were born to rule, dominate, and the troop needed their pure blood, uncontaminated by lesser genes. Any offspring resulting from the seeds of lower males would produce creatures lacking intelligence, slick-ability, cunning and other traits only the Alphas possessed.

Low Boy had no interest in destroying the myth; after all, he might become an Alpha himself one day. But he did wonder. He wondered why the Alpha females kept eyeing his horn, looking him up and down as if he was something good to eat. They had this way of beckoning with their eyes, not exactly a wink, but something between a coquettish glance and an eye rolling come — on. He was puzzled. What were they trying to do, get him killed?

Once when Alpha Number Three caught him smiling back he knocked him down and proceeded to beat on him like he was a female or some other type of low life.

But the females never stopped flirting so finally Low Boy decided to consult with one of the senior apes that once was an Alpha himself, until he lost his steam and couldn't cut the mustard anymore (so to speak). Got himself demoted, reduced in rank, only able to hang out with the kids.

"Why they be flirting all the time? With all them top shelf Alphas to choose from! What they want with me?"

The old dude, by the name of Crumpet, scratched his head, took Low Boy by the hand, sort of father-like, and led him over to a quiet spot surrounded by bushes and tall grass where they wouldn't be heard. After making sure no one was near, he gave Low Boy the following explanation:

"Just because they're Alphas don't mean they can satisfy all the various and peculiar appetites females have from time to time. Ever so often they want something different, that's all. Further more them Alphas got so much else to do-like fighting off invaders, chastising loud mouthed females, and with keeping the harem happy, often they be plain old tired".

"Now Alpha females ain't got all that much to do; laying around, getting serviced only when they feel like it, concocting up headaches when they don't, and generally acting like Miss Ann (or is it Ms. Thang nowadays?)."

"What you got to understand is that timing is everything. You got to be available when the Alphas ain't. Then you can sneak a little piece and if the ladies like your stroking, next time they'll let you know when it's safe."

Low Boy, looking unsure and confused, tried to decide if Crumpet was lying or jiving or maybe playing a trick.

"You sure that's the way it goes? I ain't never seen you getting none lately."

"Course you ain't. That's the point. That's what I'm trying to explain. Ain't nobody supposed to know except you and the lady. And she only confides in a few real close friends. Otherwise all types of unusual and dangerous hell would be breaking out all over the troop. And don't you repeat what I told you cause if you do I'll call you a lie in public and kick your ass to boot. I'm just answering your question, being friendly like an elder is supposed to."

Crumpet peeked once more through the bushes, making sure the coast was clear. Then made a scoot back to where the troop was playing chess. He whistled a jaunty tune like he had nothing but harmonious thoughts in his head.

Low Boy stayed to himself for a spell, pondering what he had heard. Them flirty females sure were looking good and his maturing sexual urgencies were getting to be a real problem.

What did he have to lose? Getting beat was happening anyway. And he remembered what he had once heard his grandfather say: "It's a poor ass that can't take an occasional kicking."

But he had always practiced caution, considering his station in life; he didn't take many chances. Normal, run-of-the mill chastising was one thing; but to go out of your way for some extra thumps. He'd have to weigh the risks and maybe come up with a plan and between weighing and planning a scheme emerged as to how he could get the Alphas to leave their territory on a mission they couldn't refuse.

First thing he'd have to do was make friends with the group of bad, unattached chimps who hung out in a thicket down the road, outside the Alpha's territory, plotting a takeover.

He began to make frequent trips using various ploys and deceptions, bringing gifts of food and conversation. He got to be so friendly and accepted that they recruited him as a sort of spy or part time scout. His assignment was to determine the physical condition of the Alphas, locate weak spots and stir up confusion.

There were only six dudes in the renegade's group but they were fit and ready, knew they were bad but not stupid: Spoils ain't never gone to losers. But becoming top dogs would mean that everything in the territory would belong to them.

Low Boy was quick to take the job; it fit in with his own plans. Without appearing obvious he began to spend more time hanging out near the Alpha's special meadow, known as the retreat, offering to buy them beer, scratch their backs and sweep up the mess they were always making. His servile demeanor made them complacent and trusting. The Alpha's observed that If he was what the next generation looked like, it would be a long time before they would be challenged.

Soon they cut back on their training, quit jogging, slept late and neglected the ladies. Although no longer in peak condition they could still rumble. It was however, a situation that allowed Low Boy to initiate the next phase of his plan.

One day he made some excuse about needing to meditate and went down the road. The roving band of six were waiting for his report.

"Them Alphas is out of shape and over the hill; females complaining about not being taken care of properly. They keep asking, 'what's up with these washed up jocks?' This would be the perfect time to take over. All I want for myself is a few choice pieces. You all can have the rest."

The elated six began jumping up and down, giving each other high fives in joyful anticipation of all the good stuff soon to be theirs.

"Now don't come in to soon," Low Boy cautioned. "Give me enough time to get them drunk or at least feeling loose and lazy. I'll start serving them beer about nine o'clock, right after breakfast. When they get to be really feeling mellow I'll come back and let you know."

Low Boy's announcement received mixed reviews and suspicious frowns. He decided he had better re-phrase and clarify what he meant.

"I ain't trying to give no orders or nothing like that. We need to be cautious, that's all."

The renegades had their own leader by the name of Roonadell. He decided Low Boy could be trusted and allowed him to leave.

When he got back he walked solemnly towards the Alpha's retreat with a pensive look as if the meditation had elevated him to a blissful state of consciousness.

It was getting late and the troop was preparing to bed down for the night. Low Boy checked his supply of beer and took a few cold ones for the Alpha's inner circle. After he'd served a round, he requested permission to share some news.

"While I was strolling along in my con- templative mood, I just happened to stray over to where them interlopers was shooting dice, just like they had nothing better to do." He waited to see if he had their attention.

Feeling their eyes glued in his direction, he continued.

"You all know, I ain't one for telling tales out-of-school, but what I heard needs to be shared, for the safety of the troop!"

Everybody knew who Low Boy was talking about. Wasn't but one group stayed down at that part of the road.

"What they was saying is that tomorrow, right after lunch, they gonna come up here and kick some ancient hind parts and take over. They say that you been on top too long and you just a bunch of has-beens."

Watching their reaction Low Boy cringed. The Alphas were upset. Alpha Number One named Dandowin got up from sitting on his heels and walked around with his arms folded behind his back, looking stern. He raised a hand to quiet the group and began to speak.

"This ain't the first time we been challenged by idle upstarts, and we ain't hung on this long by being chicken. As for being over the hill, I don't know about the rest of you but I am as bad as I ever been, maybe better. How do the rest of you feel about your own manhood? Ain't we still the cock of the walk? Ain't our females happy? You ever see any of them sashaying down the road to get their needs satisfied? Course not! And it won't be happening unless you all don't feel like Alphas anymore."

He began to gazed in the air with arms raised, gesticulating like he was talking to the Supreme Alpha with certainty of purpose, but unsure of where he lived.

"Being top dog is a feeling, a natural spark that makes you walk tall like you is somebody. We were born with this grace, this divine blessing. It can't be bought, rented or borrowed unless we agree and allow it to happen. Just cause they down there acting mannish don't mean they got what it takes." The troop listened with silent attention.

"Ain't but one way to have the spark: being born with it! But you can let some low life steal it from you. So what you all gonna do, just let 'em take it".

Angry and alarmed the troop responded with pouting and raised fists. "Who do they think they messing with, some chumps? We ought to get on down there right now! No need to delay"

Low Boy, thinking about his long range plans, tried to suggest a cautious approach.

"You all could do it right now, with ease. But why not teach them a real lesson, with no chance of a rematch? A spectacular victory would be a global warning to all others who might challenge your right to rule. Can't you visualize the press report? `Legitimate authority puts arrogant militants in their place. Peace reigns in the fields and treetops!' For years to come no one would dare challenge conventionality."

After hearing Low Boy's comments, the troop cooled down. An air of calm and confidence returned. It was decided that a good nights sleep was the best preparation. And so, after a few ceremonial stretches and ape-like yawns, off they went to their favorite sleeping places. Evening shadows crept over their habitants. Soon the sun slipped quietly below the horizon. All that greeted the darkness was occasional snoring and the minor mutterings of sleeping warriors dreaming of tomorrow's triumph.

Meanwhile Low Boy, who had been faking a snore, listened attentively to determine if all were asleep. Being satisfied he crept from his pallet and headed up the road. A strange elated feeling of intrigue and excitement energized his spirit. He pondered the situation. He was scared but damn! This was fun! What's the worse that could happen? The Alphas would win or be defeated. In either case, he'd be better off. Whoever came out on top would be in his debt. He began to chuckle. Either way I win!

When Low Boy came upon the renegades they were practicing attack positions, sharpening their teeth and wearing camouflage uniforms made from trees branches. "I see you're getting ready", he observed, "but you won't need them suits. They gonna be so hung over all you got to do is show up. Won't be much resistance. Just bust in and watch them scamper. The ladies be smiling with anticipation. No need for anymore training. Don't want to leave the fight in the gym, do we? Get some rest, save your energy, just in case."

As they gradually ended the exercise the renegade leader, Roonadell, took center stage and started chanting a secret mantra unique to their species. He lowered himself to a sitting position and sat on his heels, breathing in and out a sound resembling a low-pitched hum or a vibrating Z. The others sat as in a trance. The sound gradually diminished. Low Boy took this opportunity to plant a subliminal message, "Don't attack before one, not before one", and so on. When all were captured in a deep sleep, Low Boy took off. He returned to his sleeping place back at the Alpha's retreat and thought about the next phase of his plan: No beer with breakfast, after which they would have their usual pep rally to get the blood hot and pumping and then depart for the battle with the up starts. He wouldn't be leaving with the warriors; only Alphas had that privilege.

While they were gone he'd check out them winks. Were they for real or only idle female flirtations? Did Crumpet have the score right or was he suffering from old age dis-remem-bering?

Low Boy joined in the enthusiastic cheer-ing until the Alpha's were out of sight. Almost immediately he noticed a look of relief among the females. They began to shake hands and hug each other and formed little dancing cir-cles. With curiosity and anticipation, he lis-tened in on their conversation.

"I'm so glad they be out of here. Now *we* can have some fun!"

"Hope they be down there fighting till this time next week ."

"I hope they lose. We could sure use some new blood around here. That old stuff's too tired. Look at them puny babies we got last season."

"I know what I'm gonna do. You know that young stud stays by himself over there on the hill? Well l guess I'll wander over, sort of by accident, and see what happens. See y'all."

Other females began slipping away, all except one. She was smiling at Low Boy, eyes twinkling and looking demure. She moved closer and began stroking his back, all the time humming a flirtatious ditty.

Low Boy, feeling a delicious quiver along his spine, relaxed and closed his eyes. Then he felt himself being pulled by the hand towards a nearby cluster of bushes. When they were out of sight, they began to caress each other, which soon led to feverish fondling. Finally she turned her rear towards him and he mounted, stroking as if this was his first, and maybe his last piece. They kept at it until both were dog tired; then they rested, nestled in each other arms, satisfied and content. Low

Boy soon drifted off to sleep, dreaming about when he could do it again.

Suddenly, cheers coming from the Alpha's retreat awakened him. His companion was nowhere in sight. The shouts were an indication that someone had been victorious, but who? He hurried back and joined the others. His companion was standing some distance away with a peculiar smile on her face. She looked over at Low Boy only once, her smile widened slightly, and then she looked away and continued clapping with exaggerated wildness.

It appeared that the old guard had won. They stood in the center of the clearing, telling war stories about unmatched bravery and cunning, superior strategies and resourcefulness.

There were, however, signs that the battle had been intense. Bloody wounds were visible; movements were tortured and slow. It wasn't long before all they really wanted was to drink a little beer, attend to their wounds, and rest.

They settled into drinking and hardly noticed the females were still smiling in a strange fashion that seemed to have nothing to do with their victory, acting like they also had won something. While the chief Alpha Dandowin began surrendering to sleep, female Alpha One was staring dreamily at the ground, fingering the leaves on a twig, as if they were coins of enormous value, and smiling (actually it was more like a sheepish grin). The chief thought for a moment about the fickleness of women, but he was too tired to investigate further and was soon lost in the dreams and pain of victory.

Low Boy, consumed in his own thoughts, was also smiling and formulating his next move. The old guard has won today, but time was on the side of the renegades. They would learn from this encounter and be better prepared next time out. Low Boy could never be an Alpha without allies and the renegades were his best chance. Should he join them or stay put, biding his time?

As he thought about the future, a soft tap on his shoulder interrupted him. He turned and saw his afternoon companion, smiling and looking innocent and delectable. He took her by the hand and, together, they went off into the bushes. He'd finish his plans later.

DECOY

Felix Overmeyer, the Chief Buyer for Stein Brothers department store and Assistant Manager in charge of public image, was busy hurrying about in his usual apprehensive manner, and wondering if everything would be in order. Each department's displays would be inspected by him in keeping with his private notion that he alone possessed that rare combination of aesthetic judgment and practical wisdom sufficient to make the final evaluation. He hoped one day to be in charge of store-wide security.

At the Jewelry Department he looked through the glass of the display case and scanned the items being arranged in neat patterns on the shelves and in velvet lined boxes. He barely heard the scurrying of other busy people throughout the store, preparing their own racks and counters, anticipating the ten o'clock opening.

"Very satisfactory Miss Johnson, as always."

"Thank you Mr. Overmeyer. Hope we have a good day." She smiled, attempting to mask her true feeling. His presence always affected her studied composure although he never directly gave cause for concern. Her work was more than satisfactory. She knew that. But he always seemed to linger longer than necessary. Overmeyer tapped the glass counter-top near her folded brown hands with his frosty pink fingernails. She wore a lavender smock and a white kerchief tied in a loose fold about her neck, the prescribed uniform of the jewelry department.

Overmeyer checked his watch before moving to the hosiery section and it's kelly green costumes. In twenty minute he needed to complete the inspection of all the remaining departments, but as always, he knew he would finish in time.

Ten minutes after opening the store became a maze of humanity in motion: every department hummed with activity. Overmeyer stationed himself near the front entrance and observed each patron as they entered, confident of his ability to evaluate each in terms of important qualities that determine character, substance, and illusive intangibles he chose to call inner worthiness. In his mind he analytically coded those who attracted his attention.

The matronly lady In the stylish straw hat and carrying an alligator purse was quality for sure. The young mother in the fashionable linen suites, wearing a pearl necklace with matching earrings was a spender without question.

The ruddy-faced man with the gray mustache: a rich aroma of smoke coming from a black Havana cigar, revealed substance. Not a college man but well off. The watch chain with the solid gold Kiwanis key draped across his vest settled any doubt.

Even the young man, fingering the center button on his brown flannel suit, displayed his worth to the knowing eye of Mr. Overmeyer - short blond hair, clean shaven, pleasantly intense, reflecting ambition, a future account to be cultivated.

Suddenly Overmeyer was cut short in his evaluations as he saw, coming through the front entrance, a young black male wearing in place of a shirt, a yellow and green striped, loose fitting garment. He walked straight up to Overmeyer who felt a compelling surge of apprehension.

"Say, my man, where's the men's department?" His tone was almost friendly.

"Why - a - it's on the second floor. Is there anything I can help you with? Something in particular you're looking for?"

"That's okay man, I know what I want. I can find it myself."

He made some sort of a parting gesture with his hand, a kind of half waving salute-like movement, flamboyant and exaggerated, as if it were the distorted remnant of some long forgotten ritual of leave taking.

The figure boarded the escalator. Overmeyer followed at the proper distance required for professional observing. His analytical mechanism registered trouble.

On the second floor the young man headed for the furniture department. Overmeyer followed and noticed he was also wearing a multi-colored skullcap made of brocade or knitted material and carried a large suede bag with a woven strap slung across his shoulder. He wondered what it contained. Bones? Tools? Political literature? Merchandise pilfered from another store?

Overmeyer saw visions of jungle treachery. Dusty shadows and ivory caches being secreted away at darkest night. Images of exotic costumes and heathen principles, incorrect and out of place.

'Forget the speculation! Keep your mind on your works. Don't let yourself get distracted!' Overmeyer often had to caution himself about drifting into reveries and deserting reality in times of stress, and when faced with an unpleasant situation.

The skullcap lingered in the china department examining stem wear and a milk glass cream and sugar set. Overmeyer thought he saw him fingering the brass latch on the suede bag while the other hand continued to inspect various items. He considered the logic of moving closer, the better to observe.

Before he could decide the figure was moving again through the notions department, turned left at men's clothing and headed straight to the rack of expensive leather coats.

Overmeyer's apprehension grew to panic proportions and what he did was walk too fast, almost revealing his concern. But the busy figure didn't notice.

Backing away slowly to a suitable distance, Overmeyer regained control of himself. He wondered if it was possible to put a leather coat in the suede bag.

The figure seemed to be checking the sleeve length of a black leather coat by holding the cuff with one hand and pinching the shoulder with the other. Then he stepped back and, looking from end to end, viewed the entire arrangement as if coming to a decision. Finally he turned and walked in the direction of Overmeyer who stepped aside to the nearest counter as if making some necessary adjustments to merchandise.

"You ain't got my size man. See you later." He boarded the escalator; Overmeyer followed only to see him head straight out the door.

A properly grateful Overmeyer returned to his station to enjoy a relief so magnificent that he hardly noticed the departure of the young executive in the brown suit.

The blond young man, holding tightly to an attaché case, crossed the street and proceeded to a nearby corner where yellow shirt was leaning against the side of a building and smoking a pipe.

Seeing him the blue-eyed, brown suited gentleman broke into a pseudo walk, dipping his right shoulder with each step and holding his right arm slightly extended to the rear with the hand curved.

When he reached the corner he extended his hand, palm up for the brotherly greeting. Yellow shirt responded by slapping the palm and then extended his hand for the return slap.

"How'd we make out Bee Bee?"

Bee Bee glanced cautiously about before opening the case containing pocket calculators, tape recorders, and cameras.

"Look-a-here J.C! Man we cleaned up! This case is damn near full."

"Not bad my man, but them calculators ain't worth much. You can buy them anywhere for about eighteen dollars, which means we can't get more than ten, unless we luck up on a dummy."

'What you mean cheap? Look at them price tags. Don't that say thirty-nine dollars and ninety-five cents? I can read you know." An indignant Bee Bee pointed an accusing finger at J.C.

"Don't be knocking my score man! You wouldn't be trying to cheat me would you?"

"Listen man, can't I teach you nothing? That tag's just for suckers. The fake price. It don't mean nothing." J.C. shoved the tag up in Bee Bee's face.

"Here's the real price, them numbers in the corner. Can't you remember what I told you?"

"Oh Yea, I forgot about that."

With Blue Eyes becomming sorrowful, J.C. relented.

"Don't worry about it man. These other items is real groovy stuff. Four Canon cameras wow! At least two hundred, and these tape recorders, another hundred. Not bad for a half hours work. So with our usual split that's about two hundred for me and one hundred for you. OK?"

"OK J.C. but I still don't see why we can't split fifty-fifty." Now it was J.C.'s turn to get upset.

"You know damn well why, Honkie! Cause I been arrested for loitering and trespassing and charged and tried and acquitted three times in the last two months and you ain't so much as gotten spoken to! That's why! Cause I got to spend time going through all them court hearings and getting cleared of trumped up charges while you home sleeping. That's why! Remember this partnership was your idea, seeing as how you understand the Caucasian mentality better than I do."

"Don't go getting your Indian blood up brother man." Bee Bee attempted conciliation.

"Ain't no harm in asking. The split's OK, just lost my head for a minute."

JC cooled. "Better close the brief case before somebody figures out what's happening. Let's get out of here and go see the fence."

Looking like lawyer and client on their way to court Bee Bee and J.C. were hardly considered an unusual pair on the downtown streets. Even the conversation that passed between them aroused little suspicion. Bee Bee was making small talk about going hunting with his father and how an artificial bird could be placed on the water in order to attract the real game. In spite of the lack of natural movement, it always seemed to work.

Meanwhile Mr. Overmeyer, back at the store, continued patrolling the aisles with an air of contentment; surrounded by a warmth very much like the feeling of putting on fresh socks. This was his terrain, his world and he was completely in change. He looked forward to the end of the day and having a quiet dinner at his favorite restaurant. What would it be-roast beef with fresh green beans and tomato salad; Oyster Benedict?

As he approached the camera department he heard a scream. "They're gone! My cameras are missing!"

Turning toward the agitated voice he could tell that Mrs. Joyce Krowanski was seriously upset, opening cabinets and searching through boxes.

"What's missing, Mrs. Krowanski? Did you say cameras?"

"Yes, yes, and some other stuff."

"Calm down, we'll look together. Where were they when you last saw them?"

"Right here on top of the counter". She paused long enough to press a button that sent an alarm throughout the store. Guards rushed to the front entrance. The store manager left his office on the second floor to see what was the problem; customers thought the bell was a fire alarm and were trying to leave. The manager got the details from Mrs. Krowanski and became angry.

"This wouldn't have happened Overmeyer if that new scanning system had been installed. Nothing could get past the entrance without setting off an alarm; but you convinced me it wasn't necessary. Now see what happened!"

Overmeyer tried to explain but the manager was already on his way back to his office. "We'll begin installation immediately after closing."

That evening Mr. Overmeyer didn't enjoy his dinner. He wondered about his future.

Within a month he was moved to a new position-Vice President in charge of fashion changes. He enjoyed his new situation, (which was more like being kicked upstairs) but he missed being amongst the customers, on the floor, supervising the sales crew.

When the new system went into operation shoplifters were caught at the door, a buzzing sound alerting the guards. Replaced by an electronic device no bigger than a nickel, Overmeyer gave up his ambition of being in charge of security.

Most puzzling was the type of persons being nabbed, quality customers who would have gone unnoticed if he were still on the job. He could only conclude that times had changed and class was more difficult to determine; in his new position, only changes in fashion were his concern.

But he continues to believe his methods were sound and one day he decide to see if he could pass his own test by shoplifting at a nearby store. He would take nothing of great value- only a small concealable item. He slipped a bottle of cologne in his pocket one was only thirty feet away when he heard a demanding voice.

"Hey you, I need to see what's in your pocket!"

"What pocket? What are you talking about? Can't you see who I am?"

"I know what you are, buddy-boy; just another well dressed shoplifter, that's what."

Overmeyer reached into his back pocket and pulled out his wallet. "Look at what I have in there. Do you think I need to steal?"

"That's what they all say; stealing is like some kind of game for you people. Come on, give it up."

"That's all it was, a game. I was only testing your security system."

"Maybe so, but it looks like the system passed and you failed."

"But I didn't hear any bell or buzzer."

"That's the beauty of it; we have a silent system; no bells, just a flashing light. Come along now; lets get this over with."

Overmeyer was not arrested because the object's value was so small. He was however, ordered to stay out of the store (unless accompanied by his mother). He wasn't use to being made fun of and left the store puzzled and dejected.

Later at an office party, with everyone feeling the affect of alcohol, he told of the incident but no one believed him.

"Overmeyer you've had too much to drink, concocting a story like that. Got any more tall tales?"

Feeling lightheaded and giddy, Overmeyer joined in and laughed along with the other disbelieving revelers. The more he wondered about the incident the more hilarious it became. What was he thinking of and how was he discovered? Were there clues, some indicators of which he was unaware? Was there really a silent button or was it something else that gave him away? He never would have suspected anyone with his cultured demeanor of being a petty thief.

Overmeyer walked home in a cloud of confusion as if the world, his world at least, had turned very much around leaving him dumbfounded.

But it wouldn't last. Things have a way of righting themselves. Those who count will retain their status; the others would continue to be obvious and easy to recognize.

RANDY THE RELUCTANT

Once there was this rabbit by the name of Randy who lived in the land of foxes. It was a beautiful place with lush hillsides, clear flowing streams, meadows with abundant clovers, and Randy's favorite food, delicious strawberries. It was called Fox Hollow and being in such close proximity required constant vigilance. The Rabbits never knew when the foxes might pounce on them. Most of the rabbits knew this except Randy who suffered from a peculiar lack of perception.

The rabbit's homes were underground burrows with several back doors for easy escaping. Randy didn't even bother to learn the escape routes. Whenever the alarm sounded he simply froze in his tracks. He couldn't understand why he had to be somebody else's dinner. It seemed so unfair and he worried a lot. He noticed that squirrels ate nuts; most birds ate seeds and sometimes worms, and even the snakes didn't need rabbits for food. Often he wished he could fly away from danger just like the birds.

When he was a little baby his mother tried to teach him the reality of being a rabbit and the menacing ways of foxes. "Foxes would rather eat rabbits than anything else in the world. You must be fast and alert in order to survive!"

Randy listened and the more he listened and tried to learn the sadder he became.

"Oh what a cruel and unjust world we live in," he said to himself and to anyone else who would listen. "Why must there be foxes? What a wonderful world this would be without them."

"Never mind why" his daddy said. "Learn to cope with it or you'll never grow up to be a big bunny like your daddy. If Foxes are so great why are we still around, multiplying, and enjoying good rabbit stuff? Foxes are vulnerable too; they don't know everything."

"Couldn't foxes learn to eat strawberries or even carrots, like we do?" Randy asked, but everybody thought it was a silly question.

"Foxes eat meat, Fool! Rabbit meat like they always have, and there ain't no chance of them changing anytime soon"

Early each morning, as was their custom, all the rabbits left for the training field, except Randy. He stayed at his burrow growing fat and he missed the cunning exercises and the speed drills practiced religiously by the other rabbits. .They included fast starts, quick turning and a still standing avoidance technique known as the freeze.

While they were gone he began to wonder if there weren't some good foxes. "They can't all be rabbit eaters. Maybe they could be converted to a different way of thinking or at least induced to change their diet."

But how could he approach them? He could be eaten even before he had a chance to make his case which was essentially that other animals were easier to catch and that most rabbits were bony and tough to digest. He would need a disguise.

There was a cabin in the area that belonged to hunters who specialized in shooting wolves and sometimes foxes. They skinned the animals and hung the skins to dry from the porch rafters. Randy decided that if he could jump high enough to reach one of the skins it would make a great camouflage.

Because of his weight it was difficult. With his first leap he barely got six inches off the ground. He tried again and finally succeeded in pulling down a fox skin which he draped over his body. Only partially concealed he waddled over to where the foxes were resting.

His timing was excellent. The foxes had just finished eating and were lying about looking harmless. This lazy indifference allowed Randy to believe the disguise was working. He began to speak in a fox-like voice that sounded like a chicken trying to bark.

"Woof, cackle, woof."

The foxes were surprised; what in blazes was this fat little rabbit up to wearing a fox skin? Puzzled and amused the foxes looked at each other and back at Randy.

"Woof, cackle, woof!" he repeated.

One of the foxes decided to play along.

"Look here, fellas, it's one of the brothers come to visit. Let's make him welcome."

The other foxes began singing out greetings and cheering his arrival. "Come on over and give us some high fives. Can you stay for supper?" Randy hesitated. These Dudes were too friendly. "It's OK. You can be the guest of honor. Come, sit here, by the kitchen door."

With the foxes grinning and slowly moving in his direction, Randy lost his nerve. He got rid of the skin and took off. He could have been caught but the foxes were so busy laughing and rolling on the ground that he got away and returned to the log near his burrow completely exhausted.

Even though he was disappointed he had to conclude that becoming a friend of the foxes was unrealistic as well as dangerous.

That evening, deploring his situation, he cried himself to sleep and started to dream. The other rabbits were busy doing the bunny hop, a kind of festive dance utilized to celebrate a good day. The dance also developed rhythm that was thought to be instinctive among their kind.

As Randy dreamed he found himself in a world of vegetarians where wheat and flowers were eaten, as well as every type of fruit and nuts; where he could doze on his log all day without fear of being pounced upon.

But soon he heard grumbling coming from the carrot patch. One carrot in particular, was complaining about the unfairness of being snatched from the ground and eaten without even a chance to run. It was disturbing to learn that even carrots had cause to wonder about their situation.

When he awoke the next morning he continued his daily pattern of weeping and eating, lamenting and dreaming and doing little else except growing fatter with every passing day. He used his sharp claws to carve little symbolic figures on a log which had become a sort of lamentorium; a place of ritualistic weeping.

One day when the fox alarm sounded, all the other rabbits took to their heels, zipping and bounding over the meadows and up the hills to safety.

Randy tried to run - which really wasn't much in the way of anything except stumbling over his own fat feet. He managed to reach the summit of a rather small hill and rolled down the other side. His descent was stopped when he rolled up against a fence. He made a feeble attempt to hop over but was caught in mid air, by an ordinary, second string, runt of a fox. With all his fatness he sure made some good eating.

Meanwhile all the other rabbits were far away on a distant hill, eating clovers and strawberries and thinking about the evening activities of dancing and doing other choice rabbit things.

When the other rabbits figured the coast was clear they returned to their burrows. It was no surprise when they discovered the remains of Randy, which were nothing more than a few bones and bits of fur. Even in his grief, Randy's father couldn't respond to the chorus of "I told you so's". Randy had been warned often enough and there was hardly any expectation of a different ending.

However, as the story was recounted and carried to the far corners of the rabbits' domain, something happened. The image of Randy changed from that of a reluctant, overweight recluse to a gallant warrior who had stayed behind, defending the burrows. The story reached epic proportions inspiring poets and was even set to music. The lyrics went something like this:

> Randy stood his ground like a hero
>   should.
> Held the foxes at bay as long as he
>   could.
> While his friends and family took off
>   for the hills,

Randy was devoured as the foxes'
evening meal.

The lyrics suffered from a lack of rhythmic unity, were ridiculed by those who knew Randy best and were soon forgotten.

Randy's fate did however become an object lesson used to instruct other young bunnies on the folly of disregarding traditional ways of rabbit survival; that learning cunning skills is better than so much crying about your fate; that slim and trim is an ideal and effective body design.

A compromise was reached between those who knew the real Randy and those who thought he was a hero. A statue was commissioned depicting Randy as not too fat and somewhat muscular entitled: "Randy the Reluctant Hero"

KLUKE

There was this guy I knew from the neighborhood called Scamp. He had a fashionable way of dressing that was always eye catching with an appeal both subtle and dramatic.

He liked dark colored jackets, pastel shirts, silk ties, expensive looking shoes, and didn't often wear a hat except in the winter.

The ladies loved his rugged look and sensual, down turned lips, square jaw and middleweight fitness. He frowned a lot and was temperamental to a fault. But he was gracious and endearing to his friends who accepted his sullenness as part of his charm.

He loved to throw parties and even though he moved a lot, every apartment had the same unique and theatrical grace. Furnishings and decorations suggested nothing was accidental; every detail was carefully orchestrated. The living room was furnished with rattan couches and chairs, multi colored rugs and a collection of pillows.

Scamp also enjoyed decorating with natural materials including driftwood, old barrels; cut up burlap and pussy willows. Once he fashioned his own Christmas tree from a small branch placed in an oversized flower pot and decorated with a string of tiny yellow lights. After three weeks, when the branches sprouting tiny green leaves, he acquired the reputation of being slightly magical.

Magic or not, the dude could really spring dramatic. He literally floated with a kind of flare that turned ordinary efforts into something spectacular. Take for example, one of his favorite pastimes- creating costumes for masquerade parties.

You wouldn't think that a place like Buffalo, the epitome of a steel worker's town, blue collar to the core, ever had a Halloween tradition. But it was a big thing in the early sixties and cash prizes were awarded for the best costumes. Most of the affairs were held in taverns like the Plaidlocks, Pixies, Little Harlem, the Musicians' Club, and even the Urban League who hosted the annual Beaux Arts Ball. Three years in a row Scamp won first place at three of four locations. He would have made a clean sweep except that at one joint the owner's girlfriend showed up in next to nothing and won hands down, or was it hands off, well anyway... like I said, he always created his own costume, either from scratch or with the use of special props and make-up.

One year he fashioned a Dracula outfit wearing a black tuxedo and a black cape with a blood red lining. He wore gray gloves and his face was made up in clown white with black eyebrows and gray lips outlined in red. In his mouth he held a contraption that gave the affect of protruding fangs. As a final accent he carried an ebony walking stick with a golden handle.

The next year he created a caveman's outfit from an old fur coat and a wig picked up at the Goodwill. It fit like a toga and was draped across one shoulder and extended to just above the knees. He carved a club out of a three foot log, drilled a hole in one end and attached a rope. I tried to make a case that the rope didn't look authentic but he kept it anyway. However he did agree not to color the club (after all, what did cave men know about paint).

By the third year, I was getting jealous and a little salty. He was collecting all the prize money and all I was getting was a chance to take pictures and eat free joint food. So I decided to come up with something original and upstage the dude; something recognizable but unexpected.

After toying with a few possibilities I decided to make myself up as an authentic Klansman. I took an old sheet and cut a slit in the center so that it fit over my head. It covered front and back with space on both sides for arms. A pillowcase with holes for the eyes covered my head. On one shoulder I carried a cross, and on the other an old cigar box with a rope strap .It was covered with brown paper. The word "dynamite" was painted on one side.

Scamp wondered if my costume was a good idea. "It's all in fun," I argued. "Everybody likes a good joke, right?" He was busy working on his current rendition so he didn't argue much.

That year he planned to go as a mummy and was cutting up his own sheets into three-inch strips which he dyed a horrible green and covered with a gray-colored baking soda mixture that gave the appearance of underground aging. He put some of the gray paste on his face and practiced his mummy walk with one arm raised and the other held to the side, and dragged one leg as if it was immobilized. I started thinking of second place, maybe third if the naked lady showed up again.

Our first stop was the Plaidlocks, which is a joint that used to be a private social club called The Scottish Union, hence the name. It offered conversation, a quiet place to drink and jukebox music. When we arrived a few people in costumes were already there. Scamp made his usual startling entrance; and I followed behind, having decided on a sneaky approach as if trying not to be observed. I went to a table at the far end of the bar and took a seat. That's when I heard someone speaking.

"Ain't nothing funny' bout what you got on Man. I've seen the real thing riding late at night. Seen them burn their crosses and make speeches about how they be God's chosen people and who they hate and why. Seen them form a big circle around that burning cross and shooting in the air." He took a quick sip from his drink before continuing.

"Most black people stayed locked in their own homes, trying to be as safe as they could. But I crept up close, hiding in the shadows to see what was happening. So man you ain't funny worth a damn! You need to get the hell away from here!"

An uneasiness engulfed his end of the bar until the barmaid intervened. She tried to cool the situation.

"Its Ok Man. He's just playing. It's Halloween! He don't mean no harm, just having some fun."

The upset customer kept a tight grip on his drink, his anger increased as he stared in my direction.

"Fun my ass! Why don't he show his face? What's he got to hide? I'd like to see what kind of black fool would do a thing like this."

The barmaid continued playing peace-maker. "Come on baby, be nice. I bet if you ask him he'll buy you a drink. Never mind, I'll ask him for you".

She came from behind the bar and over to where I was sitting. "What you think? You want to buy that party pooper a drink?"

I reached for my wallet but the man had already started towards the door and disappeared. The bar returned to a relaxed mood and somebody put some money in the juke-box.

Meanwhile Scamp, who had become the center of attention, had missed what had been going on. The other customers were busy admiring the green and cruddy texture of his mummy apparel. Some were gingerly touching it to see if it was alive. The place began to fill up and soon he joined me at the table. We sat there drinking; Scamp with his one good arm and me, sipping beer that had somehow lost its taste.

When the voting was over Scamp had won again. I got fourth place by default because only four people were willing to compete.

As we started to leave I realized that any desire to continue partying had disappeared, but Scamp was in a hurry to get to the next joint.

"Hey Scamp, I don't think I want to do this anymore." He stopped and waited for me to catch up.

"Go home this early? With all the work I put into this get-up? Not a chance."

"After what happened back there, maybe this sheet idea ain't so funny"

"What happened? I didn't see anything."

Didn't you see that man at the end of the bar?"

"I heard someone mumbling about what happened when he was down home, but I was too busy being admired to make out what he was saying. Did you hear it?"

"You bet I heard it! He was talking right at me. Says he's seen the real thing."

"What are you talking about man? What real thing?"

"A real Klansman, that's what!"

Scamp was finally getting the picture. "He's probably lying or drunk. Don't pay him no mind."

"Let's give it up Scamp. No telling what could happen if somebody else gets salty at the next joint". Realizing that I was serious he offered a compromise. "

OK, let's make only two more stops."

"No, man! That dude has made me nervous. I ain't feeling so safe anymore."

"Just one more joint and we'll call it a night. Okay?"

"As long as it's the Musician's Club. At least I'll know most of the people there."

We reached the club at Broadway and Michigan, rang the bell, and went up the stairs. We walked through the crowd and took a seat at a table.

When the barmaid came over to take our orders she looked at me with a smile of recognition.

"Well bless my soul and call the cops. If it ain't ole Kluke himself. Ain't seen you since I left Mississippi. What you doing so far from the plantation?"

Scamp started laughing and joined in the fun. "He's just visiting for a spell and we're real thirsty. You gonna take our orders or not?"

"Wait a minute you green old thing. Can't you see I'm talking to somebody from down home? What do you want, Kluke baby? Need a rope or something? We got some pretty nice trees out back."

Scamp continued laughing. "He just out for an evening stroll, looking for a place to plant his cross."

"I don't mind him planting it. Long as he don't light it up and chase my customers away. Hope he checked his matches at the door."

She looked at me as if I was trying to disappear under the table or find a place to hide, which I was. She took our order and left.

While she was gone I decided it was a good time to disrobe or otherwise get the hell out from under my sheet, which I did. The dynamite box and wooden cross were also discarded.

When the bar maid returned she acted surprised. "What happened to the dude was with you? Did he have to go to the bathroom or something?"

Scamp pointed his green finger. "That's him, right there. He just taking a break before his next night ride."

"That can't be him. He ain't even the right color. Who ever heard of a black Klansman? Well he ain't really black. But even a light brown Kluke is hard to imagine. You all drink up, they gonna judge the costumes soon."

Scamp got up and limped his way to the center of the hall. The finalist included a woman dressed like a hula dancer and a man in leopard shorts with a real snake draped around his neck. Scamp got first prize again.

The party continued with great dance music and costumed figures prancing around and everybody having a good time. Except me. The mood was completely shattered. I became puzzled and anxious without knowing why.

I stayed at the table trying to figure out what went wrong with my great idea. Humor was supposed to be funny for its own sake. But it hadn't worked.

Costume affairs are no longer popular in Buffalo and Scamp and I soon drifted into other pursuits. Scamp went on to become an actor and a fashion designer. I escaped temporarily to law school before returning to an earlier interest in the creative arts.

As a feel for writing improved, youthful notions of humor melted away and humor was seen for what it is-a two edged sword; one side laughter and the other cruelty; that the most hilarious comedy always has a victim.

When the English Prince attended a party, dressed as a Nazi, many thought it hilarious but others were offended by his lack of historical understanding.

At a time when ribbing and put-downs have become a normal and acceptable form of discourse it may be well to consider how and why humor functions; it produces laughter and stings and also teaches a certain perception of truth; irrational stereotypes are taught with humor as well as with hate mail and the absorbed "truths" are identical. We laugh and hate within the same learning cocoon.

I began to conceive of a literary style that emphasized fantasy and misdirection as a more effective means of conveying meaning; with an intent to entertain rather than startle to the point of agitation.

The next time I decide to dress up I think I'll use something as inoffensive as a scare-crow costume or a cider barrel or a bear skin rug.

I AIN'T GONNA PLAY WITH YOU NO MORE

"Didn't you hear me Albert? You need to be leaving right now!" It was his mother calling from the kitchen. Sitting on the porch with a book and leaning against the wall, Albert tried to continue reading, pretending not to hear. .

"I don't even have enough firewood to finish cooking supper. Put that book up and get the wagon and go see what you can find!"

He laid the book aside and got up, muttering to himself. The smell of baking arroused a feeling of hunger as he past through the kitchen. He went out the back door to the basement entrance near the rear of the house and descended the stairs to look for his wagon. It should be in one of the corners; that's where it was put the last time he used it.

There were no lights in the basement. He went down the steps and along the walls until he reached the corner where the wagon was supposed to be. He groped about moving his foot in various directions, trying to make contact, but the wagon wasn't there. Comming back up the stairs he saw his younger brother pulling the wagon and circling around a lilac bush in the center of the yard.

"Heh, Roddy, I gotta use the wagon."

Roddy continued racing about as if engaged in a game of tag, pursued by the wagon which, it appeared, would overtake him at any moment.

"I'm using it!" he shouted, his face beaming with delight.

Standing near the edge of the circle, Albert tried to grab the wagon as it passed but misjudged and was struck sharply on the shin. He drew back in pain and when the wagon approached again he grabbed his brother by the shoulders and tumbled him to the ground. Roddy gazed at Albert with surprise.

Albert picked up the handle of the wagon and proceeded towards the front of the house. Roddy pulled himself up from the dirt, rubbed his eyes and began to cry. Albert could hear his bawling as he turned up the street. "I'm gonna tell Mama on you Albert. And I ain't gonna play with you no more either."

Some distance away Albert thought about what he had to do and hoped he would find what he needed. He would explore the delivery entrances at the rear of stores and restaurants. But first he would check out the five-

and-dime, only a block away. He was looking for discarded wooden crates, anything that would burn. He hurried past rows of quiet cottages where well kept lawn contained circles of flowers surrounded by borders of painted rocks; wooden windmill figures were simulating sawing wood. Some houses had signs announcing "Welcome Tourist".

The streets were quiet except for the clicking sound of the wagon wheels crossing the cracks in the sidewalk, and the night birds cry gradually fading away as they flew out of sight. Gray clouds floated across the moon creating shadows like undulating pools of darkness on the streets below.

Turning into the alley behind the five-and-dime he was overjoyed to discover a mountain of packing crates. He loaded the wagon and was soon trundling towards home.

As he approached the lights of a hotel entrance he noticed a man leaning casually against the wall near the doorway. He was watching, in idle indifference, a spider in his web near a freshly painted window frame. A minor breeze vibrated the not-so- fragile structure; tiny bubbles glistening like minia- ture pearls peppered the silken strands. The widest area of the web stretched near the top in loose triangles forming a platform. The lower structure resembled a kind of cone that circled inward, thinning and darkening as the neck narrowed. The spider had entered the tunnel then reappeared, crawling upside down. Moving towards the web's outer edge it seemed to set itself in ambush and waited. Soon a moth landed on the side of the building a few inches away. The spider crawled in slow deliberate steps, across an invisible thread before pausing on the painted window frame and prepared to spring. When the moth began to flutter, the spider, flexing its wiry legs, attempted to leap and found itself held firmly in the wet paint.

The man turned away from the scene and for the first time noticed the boy and heard the rattle of the loaded wagon. The boy looked around and up the street.

The man smiled and considered the bag he was holding. The smile broadened as he tossed it towards the boy. It landed two feet from where he was standing. Albert looked at what appeared to be a brown bag of peanuts.

"You can have them boy. They're for you."

Albert looked in the direction of the voice and heard a chuckle coming from a flushed face above a dark gray vest. The man was heavy and his stomach bulged out creating a roll of fat between his vest and belt.

"Go on, pick them up. They're yours."

Albert wavered. He was hungry and tired but he didn't like the way that fat old guy was laughing. (What's so funny about giving somebody some peanuts? The old buzzard didn't want them; he was just throwing them away.) Albert sensed that the giver expected something more than gratitude. Albert hesitated. (Damn, he's still laughing. What's so blooming funny?)

Albert looked again at the bag and at the figure leaning against the wall cracking the few remaining peanuts in his hand and tossing them into his mouth. He was huge, too huge to be challenged, except from across the street.

And the man knew he was safe; no real threat would be forthcoming, not from the skinny dark-faced kid, pulling a wagon loaded with wooden crates at seven o'clock at night. He inhaled the summer air and stretched himself and watched the tiny figure standing over the greasy package, anticipating a silly joke of no consequence.

Albert could see beyond the doorway and into the lobby where leather chairs and wooden tables were situated in quiet elegance. The interior was bathed in amber light that spilled over and tinseled the street, creating a deceptive radiance. Nothing could ever cross the threshold of the man's world. He could engage in a bit of play, a mischievous gesture to diminish the monotony of the evening without fear of retaliation.

Albert had never released the handle of the wagon. He clutched it with both hands as if to pull away. The bag was directly in front of him. He looked again at the figure and there was silence between them. What kind of game was this? Was it over or just beginning? He pondered these questions as the one across the way waited for some kind of reaction.

Albert really wanted the contents of the bag and thought to pick it up. Maybe he should pull away and not do anything, or just step on them. But then, Albert thought, it wouldn't hurt to look inside. (The old buzzard was still smiling.) Placing the handle of the wagon up against the crates he moved towards the little brown bag, each step a measured act, a compromise. He tried to appear unconcerned, though he wanted to race across the distance and snatch up the bag, devour the contents.

He didn't like for strangers to know and then to laugh; to know of the poverty that pushed him out into the night; that necessity caused him to trundle the loaded wagon pass the sparkling entrance way.

Albert had deliberately traveled the darkest streets, hoping to avoid seeing anyone familiar, especially his schoolmates. They would tease him about being out-on-the-search. But it would be a laugh of humorous sympathy rather than ridicule.

Well at least he had the wagon; it was better than the old baby buggy he sometimes used or the battered wheelbarrow he pushed when he went out with his father. He wished his father was with him now or maybe his brother. This guy would think twice before fooling with two of them. And with his father present he probably wouldn't' have thrown the bag at all.

He had heard this kind of laughter before and had come to understand that, for some, he was an insignificant shadow to be ignored or utilized, depending on the circumstances. He would grow to know the extent and quality of this perception.

Then he picked up the bag and felt the weight of it in his hand. The warm salty smell floated up towards his face as his fingers felt the contents and, for the first time, the revealing lightness, for the bag contained nothing except peanut shells, somehow retaining the tantalizing odor. Anticipation became piercing anger.

He could almost taste the peanuts as the anger settled into a milder irritation; then a new sensation, an embryonic pride that required a response, a pride that would grow in step with his manhood and never leave him free to turn away from humiliation without exacting some quality of satisfaction. And this hulk of a man would have to atone in some way. But what to do?

Suppose he had to run. He couldn't go home without the wagon. As the feeling grew, Albert noticed, for the first time, the eyes of the man. Something more than humor was there. This was not a joke but a calculated - - what? The twinkle had been replaced by a cold glare, reducing the distance between them as if they were inches apart, daring him to act.

"Don't you like it boy?"

He could feel the words across the space, hear them roaring into the night like a weight pressing down and encircling his very being.

In future years there would be other incidents sufficient to set the tone and mark the conflict as an enduring reality capable of occurring on the brightest day and in the most public sanctuaries; that these were not, in actuality, idle gestures, but the manifestations of an eerie subterranean, almost unconscious plan to weaken the human spirit. But what to do?

The man was huge but he was also fat; surely he couldn't run very fast. The bag was still in Albert's hand, the peanut odor a lingering reminder. Then it came to him. He tore the bag half way down one of its sides and rolled it up again. He drew back and threw it at the figure. It landed at his feet. Shells scattered over the sidewalk. In almost the same motion he grabbed the wagon handle and took off.

The figure looked at the shells; some had even settled on his shoes. "Come back here and clean this up!"

Albert was speeding around the corner when he heard the yelling and felt an invigorating brand of excitement. He didn't slow down until he was well away from the scene. Then he stopped and rested, savoring the feeling of vindication.

He wondered what the fat old dude was thinking now, and he couldn't help laughing to himself. "You like to play? Now you got something else to do. You can clean up the mess yourself".

Arriving home, Albert took the crates to the backyard, broke them up into pieces and took an arm full to his mother. When she praised him for being so prompt and resourceful he began to feel better. By the time the wagon was put away and his hands washed he returned to the kitchen to find his brother and father already seated. The smell of candied yams, fried corn, and pleasant conversation among family members, created a feeling of safety. But he couldn't forget the earlier incident. Not wanting to worry his mother he considered telling his father, thought better of it and settled for a dark and silent brooding. He could still hear the laughter.

Five years later at the age of sixteen Albert had grown to five foot ten inches and weighed one hundred and fifty pounds. He had developed a studied caution that he carried like an invisible shield whenever he was in "certain situations". Such was the case when he visited the same hotel answering an ad for a dishwasher and encountered the man who threw the bag, but what a shock! He was old and tired looking, his face wrinkled and dried up like a prune; he appeared so... so... (how could he be described?) He looked almost harmless, even ludicrous; and had lost weight along with the menacing glare. Albert was almost moved to pity. And he wondered what had happened. Was this the product of time? illness? aging? Albert had grown in awareness and confidence; the man had shrunk to a mere shadow of his former self. But Albert had also a different perception of reality – no one has absolute power and power is never forever. The man could still say yes or no about the job but now it didn't matter. He had lost the ability to terrify, and that, for Albert; was more than a temporary situation; it was equivalent to an end of a battle, if not the war.

When he was offered an application and a date for an interview, Albert declined and took another job. He left with the knowledge that something had permanently changed. The reality of his present perception was better than the shield but caution would always be a part of his arsenal of survival. He remembered the stories he had heard about jesters who manipulated and managed kings through wit and clowning. He wasn't about to become a buffoon but he would develop an articulate and deceptive manner, combined with strategic silence when appropriate and never revealing all of what he was and would become. Anyone wanting to play would encounter his own view of the game where the winning was not always guaranteed and losing was not forever.

NORTHERN COMFORT

Mr. Robinson didn't look forward to leaving Birmingham to make a trip to Buffalo. He remembered what the weather was like on his last visit in November a few years ago when his wife was still alive. They thought it was too early for snow but there it was – six inches already on the ground and then came the cold slashing rain. It seemed to get through your coat and under your skin, chilling like snow never could. Snow bounces off winter coats; winter rain clings and stays pat and now his sons were inviting him up north for his sixty-fourth birthday. He procrastinated as long as he could before agreeing. At my age, he thought, getting cold outdoors and losing body heat happens so quickly. No wonder he wore winter underwear until May, even in Alabama.

Many of his old friends were still living and he was able to work his farm with the help of a nephew and one hired hand. He didn't seem to have any serious female companions but he insisted there was still some sugar in the spoon.

His second son Jerry who lived in Buffalo, tried to reassure him that the weather would be okay in July, his birthday month. Still Mr. Robinson hesitated. "Even for July I ain't got no Buffalo weather clothes. What you expect me to wear?" His sons agreed that as soon as he arrived they would go straight to the mall and let him select anything he considered suitable for the climate and the occasion.

Finally, in late June, a few days from his birthday, when Alabama really heated up, he told them that he would give it a try; maybe a visit to Buffalo wasn't such a bad idea after all.

Now his sons began planning how they could show him a good time.

Ever since they had become fully-grown and married a certain quality of man-talk was allowed. He shared with them stories about women he had known as a young man; of how he could always get the ones he wanted, except for a few and what happened when he met their mother.

He gave them advice on the joy of a good marriage and how to make it work; that respect, communication, and sharing are more important than love. He admitted he was spending time with a certain lady but he didn't like to call it dating. Memories of his wife Eleanor, who had passed away eight years ago, continued. But "spoon talk" made his sons believes otherwise.

Mr. Robinson arrived on a sunny friday afternoon and was met by all of his four children. Shopping didn't take long and soon they were heading for the east side of Buffalo. He asked to be driven around town before going to his hotel room. His son Jerry tried again to persuade his father to stay with him but he insisted that a quiet room of his own, where he could get up and use the bathroom as often as he needed, was the best arrangement.

When the boys suggested a stop at the Anchor Bar for Buffalo Chicken Wings Mr. Robinson indicated that what he really wanted was something that looked and tasted home cooked. They settled for Gi Gi's and Mr. Robinson was glad to see that it was black owned, at least that's what he assumed.

Jerry, who was a regular customer, enjoyed introducing his father and showing off his brothers to all the waitresses and regular customers. His father ordered the special of the day – smothered chicken, macaroni and cheese, sweet peas, cornbread and sweet potato pie. He jokingly asked for buttermilk and when told they were fresh out, settled for coffee.

The friendly atmosphere suited Mr. Robinson just fine; reminded him of down home where people acted like they cared about each other. He lingered over the food and took his time drinking a second cup of coffee. When he began to get sleepy they headed for the hotel.

Two Adjoining rooms with a connecting door had been reserved. They gathered in the largest room for final planning of the week-end's activities.

Mr. Robinson took this occasion to announce one of his required conditions – he would be sleeping late Saturday morning; nothing should be scheduled.

On Saturday afternoon the few people who knew him could visit. Sunday would be the time for women, wives, grand children and other family members. But Saturday evening was only for the family men.

Mr. Robinson finally got to bed and his sons gathered at the bar in the lobby to talk about their jobs and family's, but mostly about what gift they could give their father. He said he had all he needed and the trip was gift enough. He had a car, his house was paid for and his retirement money and savings were sufficient. His sons soon decided what would be an exceptional gift, and departed with an air of anticipation.

Saturday evening arrived with a summer wind blowing in from Lake Erie.

Soon the men arrived. They were all dressed for a casual affair except Mr. Robertson who was wearing his new summer suit with a shirt and a tie.

Food was set up on a table family style. After dinner each took turns proposing a toast. Small gifts were presented to Mr. Robinson but the sons insisted the "biggie" was yet to come.

The setting sun dropping into the lake, as seen from their room on the sixth floor, shared its last moments. Finally Mr. Robinson was asked what was one of the things he never had or couldn't accomplish.

"Well, I never did learn how to swim. I think I would have liked that".

His third son, Walter pointed out that it was only the lack of opportunity. "You could have learned if you had the chance. We were thinking of something you couldn't get; something forbidden."

"Can't think of anything."

Jerry the youngest spoke up." I bet you ain't never had a white woman."

Mr. Robinson bristled. "What makes you think I ain't never – well – anyway – that's another story you don't need to know about."

"Come on daddy, tell us; have you ever?"

"I done told you I ain't speaking on that, so quit asking."

"OK, we won't ask but guess what your surprise is? We got this white lady wants to be with you."

"Wants to be with me? How's that, without her even seeing me?"

"Well dad, she's sort of in the business of being with men."

"You mean she's a street walker; a night woman?"

"She ain't exactly a street walker. She works right here in the hotel; we hired her for your birthday present."

"Now listen here, you' all done gone too far this time. I ain't told you nothing about wanting no white woman. What made you think I wanted to do something like that?"

"Just for a try Daddy; just for the experience."

Before he could answer the door to the bedroom opened and Gregory, Mr. Robinson's oldest son, comes in with the surprise hanging on his arm. Mr. Robinson looks puzzled but not intimidated. She is middle aged, wears a green silk dress with a slit on the side, and a hat that seems more appropriate for a summer beach. She looks around.

"Which one of you is Mr. Robinson? All of you look so handsome; anyone of you could be the birthday boy, I mean the birthday man."

Jerry points to his father. "That's him over there."

"Oh my, aren't I the lucky one! Mr. Robinson my name is Sally and I'm pleased to meet you. Is it okay if I sit down next to you?"

"You can sit down, but that's about all we gonna do."

Sally looks a little puzzled. "You don't mind if I have a little of your wine do you?"

Gregory fills a glass and hands it to her. Sally looks at Mr. Robinson who remains cool and non-committal. Sally smiles in his direction.

"I hope we can have a good time together and I can help to make this a real special party on your- how old are you today?"

"I'm old enough; maybe too old for what you got in mine"

Sally begins to get nervous. "But Mr. Robinson, I really need the money. Of course if you don't like me or can't do it ... It's okay."

"I ain't said nothing about not being able, I just thought ... well maybe we can go into the other room for just a while; but don't expect to much."

Sally perks up, grabs him by the hand and heads toward the bedroom. When they leave the sons are excited and surprised that their father went for it; wondering what he was doing and how the girl would approach her "responsibilities". Would she be able to arouse his interest and what would it take; would he be willing and able to go along with the program and enjoy his gift?

The youngest son Jerry suggested that they take a little peek but the idea was rejected as being too uncool.

It seemed forever but finally they returned. Their father looked a little sheepish and the girl seemed elated. She tries to straighten her skirt while he toys with his tie. Sally seems anxious to talk.

"I ain't had such a good time with an older gentlemen in so long, I'd almost forgotten what it was like".

Gregory tries to pay her but she protests.

"No, no, that's too much. Just give me half, that'll be enough." Gregory insists that she take it all; she hesitates and seems to want to linger. She waves goodbye as he ushers her out then Jerry turns to his father who starts a slow, quiet laugh.

"Why you laughing Dad; what happened?"

Dad laughs louder. "Where did you find that woman? She seemed so awkward and new at this. Kept asking for instructions, 'am I doing it right; is it ok? ' Don't they have schools for prostitutes up north?"

"But how was it?"

Dad finally stopped laughing. but continues a peculiar smile,"

That was the most *or-din-ary* piece I ever had; weren't nothing rare about it. You call that a special birthday present? Forbidden fruit? Ought to be turned out to pasture for more seasoning, that's what I think."

"Wasn't it different?"

"Not so much different as dull. Can't she make a living doing something else?"

"We thought this would be a unique experience."

"Unique ain't the word; un-neek's more like it. I hope I didn't hurt her feelings; she had me so close to laughing; I could hardly hold it in."

Jerry, unable to contain his excitement, asked again.

"Can't you share some details Daddy?"

"No, I ain't sharing; I ain't never talked about a lady afterwards and I ain't gonna start now"

Mr. Robinson returns to his seat and seems to be in deep thought."

"Is that what they been trying to keep us from all these years? If we had only known. Oh well, what we gonna do next?" The question catches them by surprise; nothing additional had been planned beyond the big event. And no one could come up with anything else to do.

Since the party had reached its peak, and Mr. Robinson needed to get some sleep it was decided to call it a day.

Before leaving, they talked a little about tomorrow's plans and Mr. Robinson was soon in bed. He smiled as he reviewed what had happened– (no need to think anymore about integration.) He slept soundly, pondering all the while if he had raised his sons properly, and wondering what his down home friends would think about his "gift". A smile never left his face.

THE WAY OF DREAMS

Ruthie awoke on September 12th determined to go to her job, but something seemed to be holding her back. Nine eleven would be remembered by all Christian Americans and she believed she was one of them. She lived in a stylish apartment in a fashionable neighborhood and was treated as if she belonged.

All day on the eleventh she had stayed glued to the television numbed by the repetitive theme of vengeance, and heard for the first time the expression "sand niggers". She wondered how inclusive the enemy circle would be. Remembering her status, she was somewhat consoled; after all I am still a Christian American. Why shouldn't I be safe? And I can't remember the last time someone called me nigger. Slowly she dragged herself from under the silk sheets on her king sized bed and stepped on the plush carpet. She felt pampered and protected as she looked about her bedroom decorated with contemporary African paintings and wood carvings. Her bed was covered with a mud-cloth spread. She removed her flannel night gown and made her way to the bathroom; the blue tile sparkled as the lights were turned on. The smell of a lemon-vanilla body wash filled the air. She welcomed the thought of a leisurely shower and climbed in, full of expectation. The soothing needles of warmth titillated her body. She washed with closed eyes, imagining herself on an African beach, and emerged refreshed, dried herself with a fluffy terry-clothe towel and began the task of getting ready for work.

An African head wrap, which had become a kind of trademark as well as an ethnic statement, would always be included. There were several to chose from. Finally she chose a green and brown color combination that matched her knitted dress made of a soft beige fabric. A gold bracelet and a cowry shell necklace completed her selection. She felt comfortable and correct and remembered to take along the book she had started reading. It would keep her company at lunch.

On the way to work she stopped for coffee, took it with her on the elevator and noticed for the first time an unusual silence. It continued along the corridor, followed her through the office and to her desk. What was going on? People were gathered in small groups, engaged in nervous conversations.

She worked at her desk until lunchtime and went quickly to the cafeteria, carrying the book, but today she didn't want to eat alone.

A short distance away co-workers occupied a table. She decided to make a move. After all, she was the same as they, felt the same sense of outrage, the same patriotic zeal and the need for a show of unity. She put the book in her purse, picked up the tray and walked in their direction, and sat down at one end of the table without being noticed, until she spoke.

"How you doing?" They seemed startled to hear her voice. "Isn't it terrible that they would do such a thing to us, to innocent people?" No one answered immediately but soon she heard someone speak.

"It's because they think we're weak and won't fight back. They're just a bunch of uncivilized cowards; the heathen bastards!"

Angry agreement resounded around the table as they studied her with a peculiar and unfamiliar intensity.

"Why are you sitting with us? You've never done that before. What's so different about today?"

She hesitated before responding.

"This is the first time we've shared a common tragedy and, to be honest, I didn't want to be alone, not today. I hope you don't mind."

They were all females from various European cultures yet Ruthie had never felt a sense of sisterhood with them. But she reminded herself that, after all, they were all Christian and American, and she was as well educated as they. She continued to be the center of their collective focus.

"Why do you wear that thing on your head?" Ruthie was startled at the hostile frankness. "What thing?"

"That turban with the gaudy colors! What is it anyway?"

"It's an African wrap;. I wear it all the time."

"Yes we noticed. But do you have to wear it to work?"

Ruthie was becoming irritated.

"I didn't come over here to talk about the way I dress. I just thought ..."

"Is the middle east part of Africa? How many Black Americans are Muslims?" The questions were coming too fast; she wasn't prepared.

"I-a-don't know much about Arabs or Muslims. I'm Christian and African American, that's all. I wear this head wrap because it represents my African heritage."

"Why aren't you just an American like the rest of us?"

(I would be, if you let me), she thought, but wouldn't say the words. Something about their intensity seemed to overwhelm her.

"All I know, or at least I hope, is that some good will come from all of this. It's an American tragedy. We all feel it. God will not allow this horrible deed to go unpunished. Maybe this will cause prayer to be returned to the public schools."

"Maybe we should go back to neighborhood schools. I always liked that better- my own school in my own community with my own kind".

Ruthie felt an overwhelming urge to get up and leave but pride and increasing anger made her stay. She struggled to further explain how her feeling must be the same as theirs.

"Can't any of you understand? We are all in this together"

"Next she'll be asking us, can't we all just get along?"

With this final slap in the face, Ruthie decided she'd had enough.

"As long as I'm black you people can't recognize that I'm American too, is that it?"

Their only response was staring at her in frigid silence as if at a foreigner or even worse, a stranger. Ruthie picked up her tray and returned to her table. She had always believed that this was her country too and wondered what to do next.

But was it really so? Was she really a full citizen or something less? A feeling of loneliness and separation crept over her like a sudden chilling wind. She had cut herself off from her co-workers and also from her own people. After years of isolation, who were her people? Her life was measured by the things she had accumulated. Living alone was acceptable because of what she had; her solitary lifestyle left little time to consider the lack of human connection; after all she had that which was most important – material success. There was no one, at this time, she was expected to comfort and no one to comfort her.

She remembered having heard that there are at least two types of loneliness-missing someone or something in particular, or a vague disquieting feeling of incompleteness.

During the following days a subtle uneasiness plagued her waking hours and at night she dreamed of an empty sky where solitary clouds avoided each other, moving within their own limited circles.

Nothing at home provided the usual pleasure; everything had been reduced to just "stuff". She wondered about her family she only saw at Christmas, and of her future life. Even her plan to retire early and travel had lost its attractiveness. Without friends or children or family; without a significant other in her life, where would her comfort and connection come from when she reached middle age and even older.

Two weeks later, she discarded her African wrap but it didn't help; no one at work even noticed. She continued eating alone and observing more closely her workplace environment, paying particular attention to how the lunch time socializing was divided into many small groups. She wasn't the only one who sat by alone; others were doing crossword puzzles and listening to music from ear phones and portable players. But there was one difference; everyone else exchanged casual greetings and made small talk. She now realized her air of aloofness suggesting "don't touch" had discouraged any unnecessary contact. Living in her world, in the pursuit of success, she had felt fulfilled. And It had worked, up until now.

Pondering her situation, certain additional realities began to emerge – her internalized culture and mother country was where she had actually been born and educated, and that was America. Whatever subconscious contact she had with Africa was more of a romantic notion than a functional reality. After her ancestors survived the middle passage, European influence in Africa continued. Few social customs or cultural elements were retained intact on this side of the ocean. And what was retained had little connection to present day Africa.

She was stuck in the middle of a cultural rut; stranded between what was and what is. She was mostly American whether she liked it or not. But that was not so bad. No culture ever remains the same and neither does a people. She was what she was, an African American, regardless of limitations and incomplete definitions.

A major tragedy can become the catalyst for adaptive modifications. She had to regroup, establish new priorities, and create a better balance in her life. There was still a sliver of hope.

Her family had never deserted her and she knew the door remained open. They would consent to re-establishing their relationship.

She started the process with a surprise visit to the home of her oldest sister. It turned out that all the children were there and her mother just happened to be visiting. Ruthie was overwhelmed by the warmth and excitement generated by the impromptu get-together. It was as if their love for her had continued and a shower of tears washed her face, melting make-up and transforming her usual composure into an uncontrollable outburst of childish sobbing.

Her mother who understood, held her in a warm embrace and rocked her gently until the shaking subsiding. Her sister washed her face all the while commenting on her "messed up make-up".

Reconnecting with her family allowed Ruthie the luxury of relaxing her self-centered preoccupation and becoming more involved in what they might need. She was prepared to share with them whatever she had and was pleasantly surprised to learn they were all doing fine. All they really wanted was her, back with the family.

Attending church with her mother she rediscovered the enduring significance of her faith and recalled what it was like as a child, being moved by the gospel music and experiencing the warm connection of a church family.

There remained the problem of being an American of sorts; but what else could she be? Christianity was easy because it had little to do with race even though her mother's church was totally black.

She decided to determine her own style and level of involvement. If she had to be less than one hundred percent American there ought to be something called second-class patriotism. She would not be disloyal but absolute commitment should not be required or expected. She'd be cool with it; not overbearing but she hated to give up the wrap.

At work the next day no one could ignore what she was wearing. It was a wrap all right, and it was red and blue with white stars.

THE BUTTON

After twenty years they were able to acknowledge a total linking together and could openly speak of it, not in conventional expressions such as "closer than peas in a pod", or "like peaches and cream", but in their own unique and private manner. He would often say to her, "sometimes I can't tell where your spirit begins and mine starts, there're so overlapping." She would respond with "It's' like our minds and hearts are locked together, that's what's going on." Conversations not for public sharing and spoken only to each other.

Jealousies had ceased long ago, but there remained a need for personal time and space, which both understood and recognized, even when sitting silent together in the same room, each absorbed in their own thoughts. And they shared one final worry, as to who would go first. It was there even as they continued the habit of doing for each other. He loved to cook for her and she often bragged about the scrumptious meals he prepared.

"He's just spoiling me. I'll never be any good for no other man, if we ever breakup."

He indulged a gentle smile when she talked like that.

"It ain't nothing really, only a little something I threw together." This always made his wife giggle.

"Well you just keep on, cause it sure pleases me, whatever it is".

One of his favorite dishes was oven baked corn pudding, a recipe he learned from his father. It included fresh corn, milk, butter, pimentos, finely diced onions, and a touch of brown sugar.

What she liked best to do for him was ironing his shirts to a smooth and sparkling perfection. She didn't care for the new steam irons because the shirts came out too soft and with less of a shine. When he was cooking she often set up the ironing board in the kitchen.

"Ain't you worried about what them shirts gonna smell like?"

She smiled at his teasing and all she did was set up right in front of the kitchen fan.

"Them ham hocks and cornbread can't compete with my starch and sprinkling water. You just keep on cooking and let me do the ironing."

She ironed his shirts as if preparing a royal robe; knew exactly how to position and turn the garment, moving with smooth strokes that left a gleaming surface with the look and feel of ivory. When each was completed it was hung on a large hanger to help keep its shape. She let them cool in the kitchen before placing them in their shared closet where she could admire them whenever she opened the door.

Sunday was the primary occasion for specials dresses, shirts and ties; as were weddings, holidays, and family gatherings, And there was one other remarkable event. It was when they participated in the picketing of a downtown five and dime store, Woolworth's to be exact. They marched with a group of young student and his wife thought that if they "dressed up" others would know they weren't rough or irresponsible, like some of the others. It was something of a surprise when they got arrested, "just like everybody else." But at least they were "presentable".

When he retired from the steel plant after thirty-seven years, everyone wished him well and hoped he and his wife, Geneva Ann, would have a long and happy life. It was also the first and only time his full name – Arthur Lewis Griffin – was ever spoken at the plant.

A growing feeling of apprehension stayed with them long after the affair. They knew they were drawing closer to that dreadful day.

One morning, while ironing his best white shirt, she noticed one of the buttons was loose and about to drop off. She got her sewing box from the cupboard and went to work.

He watched her fingers moving with a familiar smoothness, pushing the needle through the buttonhole and back up again. But it took longer than he remembered and she appeared worn out from the effort. He wondered how soon it would it be.

The shirts were placed in the closet next to his black suit. He planned to leave it there until ...(he couldn't form the words, let alone speak what was on his mind).

Who would go first was settled four days after her seventy-sixth birthday. He wore the black suit but not the special white shirt. When he went to put it on he discovered the button was hanging by a single thread. He wondered if this was a final message from her and if so, what did it mean. His daughter offered to sew it back on but he refused. He didn't want anyone else fooling around with it. He tried to do it himself but did a poor job and gave up. When his daughter noticed his only comment was "Let it be, she'll understand. Can't nobody do it like her. When my time comes bury me in it like it is."

At the funeral he felt a hollow emptiness – like missing two meals in a row – but not a genuine sadness as he had expected. They had begun grieving quietly together, and sometimes separately, long before and the necessary decisions had been made. Their little bit of money and other material possessions had been divided up among the children or given to friends; no squabbling over property after they were gone. They kept only what would be needed to get them through to the end.

The children were reluctant to take anything and felt it was too soon to be giving anything away.

"How do you know how much you'll need? Are you sure you're keeping enough?"

"We'll be fine; don't worry. We've figured it out."

After the funeral, the black suit was returned to the closet. Soon his children noticed he seemed to be waiting for an expected visitor without sadness, fear or anxiety.

He kept himself busy taking care of the house and her garden. Old friends when visiting, teased him about doing yard work, which they knew he never enjoyed. He'd tease them back.

"I've been doing gardening all along. Y'all ain't never caught me at it before, that's all."

He also spent more time at the barbershop, drinking coffee and swapping lies with the old timers. It helped use up a good portion of the afternoon and informed about who had died or was sick or had moved out of town.

In the evening the challenge was how to get tired enough to sleep when he went to bed. He tried everything: walking twice around the block, sweeping the porch, raking the lawn again, reading, and drinking warm milk. It all helped a little.

Finally, through trial and error, he discovered what was most helpful – a toasted peanut butter sandwich washed down with a little wine.

Morning was the easiest part of the day. He automatically woke up at 6 a.m. and cooked the usual two eggs and since he had cut down on meat, only two strips of bacon. Grits had been replaced with fried apples. He topped it off with wheat toast without butter, coffee with low fat milk and just a pinch of sugar. His health had always been good and he planned to keep it that way but without a persuasive reason; what was he saving himself for?

One evening while walking around the block he felt a throb in his chest, like a drum beating from some place nearby. He slowed down and it went away. Probably walking too fast or too soon after eating, he thought. When the same thing happened the following evening and the next, he got checked by his doctor and was told that it was nothing serious, considering his age, but he should slow down.

"Slow down!" He eyed the doctor with amused skepticism. "If I slow down any more, I'll be standing still."

On the way home he considered maybe he should slacken his pace just a bit; spend more time on the porch in the rocking chair, dozing and watching life moving at its own pace.

When the discomfort increased, even while sitting, he really began to worry. It was as if a zipper was being pulled inside his chest and had gotten stuck along its pathway, and the effort to free itself was causing the pain.

He didn't tell his children but called more often; he asked his grandchildren to write something for him in their own hand and not on the typewriter or the computer, and when they did he taped their notes to the refrigerator. When he stopped showing up at the barbershop his friends came by more often.

One day they found him slumped over in the rocking chair. He was breathing but his pulse was weak and his hands were cold. They called for help and he was taken to the hospital where he stayed for three weeks. It was determined that he was suffering from a mild case of malnutrition. He admitted occasionally missing a meal because he didn't like eating alone. And there was little joy in the kitchen with no one to talk with.

His children, realizing how much he missed their mother, would come by to prepare the evening meal and eat with him. They invariably prepared something extra for the next day.

Even with this help he continued to lose weight and needed a cane to help him walk around. When he decided to sell the house and move into a retirement village, the worry of his children intensified. But the move seemed to be good for him; his appetite improved and he enjoyed the company of people his own age. And being around the ladies seemed to improve his memory.

He lived for another six years to the amazement of his doctors and the wonder of his children. His disposition never changed and his mental faculties remained clear except for the difficulty of remembering dates and where certain of his personal articles were "hidden away.

He viewed it all as one of life's little jokes to be tolerated with grace and humor.

He was able to visualize his funeral and make peace with what was coming. It would be simple. His few remaining friends would be there of course. He smiled to think what else did they have to do.

His coffin of dark mahogany with sparkling brass handles catches the light and bounces it off the ceiling. Within the church the smell of flowers mingling with after shave lotion and deodorants; the ladies in their special Sunday hats and the men wearing black suits and fresh hair cuts. Timid children hanging on to parents, staring into their faces, looking for guidance and assurance.

He would be wearing, for the last time, his own dark suit, and the white shirt with the button still improperly attached.

What would she say to him when they met again on the other side? Would she notice the button and shake her head at the carelessness or would she understand. Maybe she might remind him that looking presentable in public is always important even at the end. Or maybe she would tease him about being so sure only she could do it properly.

He made a game of trying to decide how he would respond.

"I could have done it myself", but she would know better. She might ask why he wouldn't let one of the children to do it.

"There just never seemed to be enough time, with them so busy". That wouldn't work either.

He knew she would be glad to see him and he could catch her up on all the family happenings, if she didn't already know. (Heaven ought to have a way of keeping folks informed and up to date).

He wondered if married folk shared the same cloud and if there was any segregation, and if so, who got separated from whom, and for what reason. What was the size of the cloud for black folk and where were they located?

The funeral was as he imagined; grieving was adequate and heartfelt; but the radiance of the weather was a surprise. It was as if his homecoming required the chirping of birds and bright billowing clouds to guide him on his way.

Soon they would be together and he would experience the unfolding of the final mystery, the ultimate, universal knowing. He departed in peace with thoughts of her.

When he arrived he became aware of a quiet beyond sensing and of a brightness without color .The idea of a reunion merged with a vague notion of eternity, and he experienced a peace as warm and gentle as a cooling flame. And finally he was surrounded by a presence that could only be the essence of his one and only.

Printed in the United States
204147BV00001B/34-84/A

9 781420 855319